# FLOOD

# FLOOD

Mary Calhoun ◇ *Illustrated by* Erick Ingraham

**Morrow Junior Books**
NEW YORK

Pastel pencils and watercolors were used for the full-color illustrations.
The text type is 15-point Aldine 401 BT.

Text copyright © 1997 by Mary Calhoun
Illustrations copyright © 1997 by Erick Ingraham

Printed in Singapore at Tien Wah Press.

1 3 5 7 9 10 8 6 4 2

Library of Congress Cataloging-in-Publication Data
Calhoun, Mary.
Flood/Mary Calhoun; illustrated by Erick Ingraham.
p. cm.
Summary: One fictional Midwest family is forced to leave
their home during the flooding of the Mississippi River in 1993.
ISBN 0-688-13919-1 (trade)—ISBN 0-688-13920-5 (library)
1. Floods—Mississippi River—Juvenile fiction. [1. Floods—Mississippi River—Fiction.]
I. Ingraham, Erick, ill. II. Title. PZ7.C1278Fj 1997 [E]—dc20 96-14836 CIP AC

To the victims and workers in the Midwest floods of 1993.
And in celebration of people in all times who unite their efforts
in the face of natural disasters.
—M.C.


For my wife, Cynthia, and daughters, Katrina and Britta
—E.I.

"Flood!" people kept saying. Sarajean stood on tiptoe, but she couldn't reach the gray line on the wall inside the fire station.

"That's the high-water mark from the Big Flood, back when your father was a baby," Grandma told her. "They don't paint over it, because it's the record."

"The river came up that high?" Sarajean exclaimed. "Can it do that now?"

"Not with the higher levee—and with your daddy and everybody else over there today, building it up even more with sandbags."

They went back to the table where Mom and some other women were making sandwiches. Sarajean spread mayonnaise on bread and listened to the talk.

"…all the flooding upstream. Just north of us the river's eight feet higher than it's ever been."

"Well, half the country is sopping wet and pouring into the Mississippi."

"Sure, it's rained nearly every day since early May. We're past the Fourth of July, and now the TV weather forecaster says the *big storm* is coming!"

Sarajean frowned. That was her beloved river they were talking about. "The river won't hurt us!" she declared.

Just then Dad and some levee workers came in, sweaty and dirty.

"How does it look?" Mom asked.

Dad gave her a muddy grin. "Good as it can. If we don't keep the river out, it's not because we haven't tried."

He washed and ate, then told Mom, "We'd better do some sandbagging at home. Rock Creek is over its banks and is spreading into town."

Outside was a mountain of sandbags. Dad and Mom loaded some into their pickup truck.

Sarajean's dog jumped up, giving eager whines.

Sarajean patted her. "Hey, can Josie and I go look at the river?"

Grandma started to protest, but Mom nodded at Sarajean. "She'll use her good sense."

"C'mon, Josie!"

They ran down the gravel road. Going to the river was what they loved best.

The sod wall of the levee was piled high with sandbags. Men and women rushed along it with straw and bags to stop water from seeping through.

Sarajean and Josie scrambled up. "Wow!" Sarajean admired the powerful sweep of the river. The Mississippi was higher and wider than she'd ever seen it.

"Yark!" Josie moved, but Sarajean hugged her close, and the dog pushed her wet nose against Sarajean's cheek.

Another truckload of sandbags arrived. A man yelled, "Hey, kid! Get down from there!"

Sarajean and Josie trotted home between cornfields standing in rainwater. They raced the storm as lightning flashed in black clouds and thunder rumbled.

Dad and Mom were stacking sandbags against the house. Sarajean helped, shoving bags off the tailgate. When the rain got heavy, they all dashed inside.

Grandma was draping damp clothes on a drying rack, and Sarajean caught Josie before she could shake her wetness on them.

Mom said, "This rain's not going to stop. Maybe we should move to Perry's until the flood gets past us." Dad's older brother and his wife, Mary, lived on higher ground a few miles back from the river.

"No sirree!" exclaimed Grandma. She dropped into her rocking chair and held on to its arms. "I didn't leave my house in the Big Flood, and I'm not leaving now!"

"Sure," Dad said, "we'll just move upstairs like you did then."

In the morning rain fell steadily as Sarajean took Josie out for her run. When they got back, she saw Dad hauling the johnboat from the backyard. "You aren't going fishing *now*?"

"Nope. Just want it handy." He tied the boat to a porch post.

Their neighbor splashed across the muddy street, and Sarajean watched as he and Dad carried out their new couch and put it in the pickup truck. Then the TV set. Then Grandma's rocker.

"Dad!" she cried. "The river isn't going to come in our house, is it?"

"Could."

"So are we leaving?"

"No, doll. We're just moving these things to Perry's barn."

Sarajean smoothed her dog's wet ears. "It'll be all right, Josie."

A sheriff's deputy came to the door while they were eating. He said, "With the heavy rains to the west of us, Rock Creek is so swollen it could be in your front door by morning. We're advising everyone to leave."

"No!" Grandma said to Dad. "Your father died in this house. You were born here. I'm staying."

Dad told the man, "We were planning to move upstairs."

"Suit yourselves, folks," the deputy said. "But if the levee doesn't hold, that Mississippi flood could float you out your upstairs windows."

Dad nodded to the deputy. "I guess we'll take our chances, at least for now." He put an arm around Mom. "We've never seen a trouble yet we couldn't handle, have we?"

When Mom smiled at him, Sarajean felt safe.

"Well," Dad said, putting on his rain gear after lunch, "I'd better get our things to Perry's. I'll leave the truck up by the highway, just in case."

"Wait!" Grandma called. "That dog can't move upstairs with us. She'd better go to Perry's, too."

"No!" Sarajean squatted and clutched Josie.

Mom knelt with her arms around Sarajean and her dog. "Honeybird, it's just until the flood gets over with."

Sarajean sobbed. The last she saw was Josie barking out the pickup window.

Sarajean stamped out her feelings on the stairs, carrying up canned foods and saucepans, ice coolers and bags of ice. Mom set up the camp stove and lantern on a chest at the end of the hallway.

At suppertime Mom fried hamburgers on the stove downstairs, and they ate at the table. Maybe cooking and eating upstairs would be fun, Sarajean thought, like camping out in their own house.

But when she reached a bite of burger down to Josie and Josie wasn't there, it was not fun at all.

That evening there were no lights in the neighbors' houses. Had everyone left but them? The hot night felt lonely, and Sarajean shivered.

She touched her river treasures on the windowsill: a polished pink stone, a sparkly chunk of geode, a shell with round holes. Grandma had told her factories used to punch buttons from river shells.

Deep in the night a crash of thunder woke her. She looked out the window to see if the river was coming. A streetlight shone on water.

Josie would be shaking with fright at the thunder. Be all right, Josie, she thought to her dog.

Later still she dreamed a jagged red line. No, it was sound outside, the fire siren wailing. A man's voice shouted on a loudspeaker, "Levee's broke! Everybody get out now!"

He kept up the cry from a car fording through water. In the yard the johnboat floated beside the top porch step.

"You don't belong in here!" Sarajean screamed out the window at the river. "How could you do this to us?"

She ran to her parents' bedroom. "We heard," Dad said, pulling on clothes. "Go wake Grandma."

Mom was telephoning Uncle Perry to say that they were coming.

When they were all in the johnboat, Dad started the outboard motor. Grandma held a bag of photo albums in her lap. "Never thought I'd leave," she said.

Sarajean held the buttonhole shell. In the early morning light she looked around at the drowning town. A turtle swam by the window of a house. You wouldn't have done this if it hadn't rained so much, Sarajean told her river, trying to forgive it.

They left the boat at the highway and crowded into the pickup. When they got to Uncle Perry's house, he was outside. "Come right in! Breakfast's ready."

Something white with black and tan patches ran past him. "Josie!" Sarajean held her dog while Josie licked and licked her face.

"Oh, you poor people!" Aunt Mary exclaimed at the door.

"Not so poor," Mom said. "Even if we lose the house, we're all still alive."

"Lose the house!" Grandma cried. "My home."

Dad led her to the table, saying, "We can handle it, rebuild if we have to."

Sarajean looked at Josie by her knee, at the dear faces around the table. "Hey, no, you can't lose your home, Grandma! Because home means us. Home is when we're all together."

Grandma sniffed, and smiled. "You're right, child. We haven't lost what's important."

Sarajean hugged her.

# EPILOGUE

Even though Sarajean and her family are fictitious, what happened to them during the flood of 1993 did happen to countless families throughout the Midwest.

After a levee broke, a town like Sarajean's was covered by twelve to sixteen feet of water. The area had already received fifty inches of rainfall since November 1992. Heavy rains continued through July and came again in mid-September. Late that month water still covered some streets.

In the devastating flood of 1993, all low ground along the Mississippi and the rivers that flow into it was flooded, from Wisconsin to southern Missouri. That summer flooding occurred also along the Missouri River from Omaha, Nebraska, to St. Louis, Missouri.

Many people chose not to return to flood-prone areas. Others, like Sarajean's family, went back to their damaged homes and businesses and restored them.